W9-APJ-414

TWO of a kind ™

To Snoop or Not to Snoop?

Look for more

titles:

#1 *It's a Twin Thing*
#2 *How to Flunk Your First Date*
#3 *The Sleepover Secret*
#4 *One Twin Too Many*

ATTENTION: ORGANIZATIONS AND CORPORATIONS

Most HarperEntertainment books are available at special quantity discounts for bulk purchases for sales promotions, premiums, or fund-raising. For information, please call or write:

**Special Markets Department, HarperCollins Publishers,
10 East 53rd Street, New York, NY 10022-5299
Telephone (212) 207-7528 Fax (212) 207-7222**

TWO of a kind ™

To Snoop or Not to Snoop?

adapted by Judy Katschke

from the teleplay written by Larry Kase
& Joel Ronkin

from the series created by Robert Griffard
& Howard Adler

≡≡ HarperEntertainment

A PARACHUTE PRESS BOOK

A PARACHUTE PRESS BOOK

Parachute Publishing, L.L.C.
156 Fifth Avenue
Suite 325
New York, NY 10010

Published by
HarperEntertainment
A Division of HarperCollins*Publishers*
10 East 53rd Street, New York, NY 10022-5299

If you purchased this book without a cover, you should be aware that this book is stolen property. It was reported as "unsold and destroyed" to the publisher and neither the author nor the publisher has received any payment for this "stripped book."

TWO OF A KIND, characters, names and all related indicia are trademarks of Warner Bros.™ & © 1999.
In cooperation with Dualstar Publications, a division of Dualstar Entertainment Group, Inc.
abc™ & © 1999 American Broadcasting Company, Inc.

Cover photo by George Lange

All rights reserved. No part of this book may be used or reproduced in any manner whatsoever without written permission of the publisher, except in the case of brief quotations embodied in critical articles and reviews.

For information address HarperCollins Publishers,
10 East 53rd Street, New York, NY 10022-5299.

ISBN 0-06-106575-7

HarperCollins®, ® , and HarperEntertainment™ are trademarks of HarperCollins Publishers Inc.

First printing: July 1999

Printed in the United States of America

Visit HarperEntertainment on the World Wide Web at
http://www.harpercollins.com

10 9 8 7 6 5 4 3 2

CHAPTER ONE

"Wow," twelve-year-old Ashley Burke gasped. "Mary-Kate, do you have any idea what the full moon looks like through this telescope?"

Her twin sister, Mary-Kate, sat on the sofa in the attic. She tossed a softball into the air and caught it again.

"Like a pepperoni pizza with extra cheese?" Mary-Kate asked. She leaned back and sighed. "Why do we have to study astronomy anyway?"

Ashley pointed the silver telescope out the attic window toward the early evening sky.

"So we can learn about the solar system," she said. "You know, get a look at planets, stars, meteors . . . "

"We can do that by watching reruns of *Star Trek!*" Mary-Kate groaned.

Ashley rolled her eyes. She and Mary-Kate were twins, but they didn't always agree on everything. Ashley loved math and science—Mary-Kate didn't. Mary-Kate loved softball—Ashley didn't. In fact, sometimes the two were as different as . . . the stars and the planets!

"You really should give sky-watching a shot, Mary-Kate," Ashley said. "You never know what you'll find up there."

Mary-Kate stood up and walked over to Ashley.

"Who cares what's going on up there?" Mary-Kate asked. She pointed out the window to the street. "I want to know what's going on down *there.*"

"Watch it!" Ashley said. She looked over her shoulder at her twin. "Don't get the snooping bug again!"

Mary-Kate put her hand to her forehead and grinned. "Hmmm. I *thought* I was coming down with something."

"Well, you're not going to do it, Mary-Kate," Ashley declared. "You remember what happened the last time we used this telescope to snoop."

"Sure." Mary-Kate shrugged. "I spotted Erin

Wood, the strictest vegetarian in school, eating a deluxe hamburger on her stoop. Then we told everyone at school—"

"And Erin hasn't spoken to us since!" Ashley finished her twin's sentence.

"Okay, okay," Mary-Kate said. "How was I to know it was a *veggie* burger?"

"It was bright green!" Ashley cried. "And when Dad found out we were snooping, he turned green, too."

Mary-Kate nodded. *"That* I remember!"

Ashley turned back to the telescope. She didn't mind using the telescope to explore outer space. She loved checking out meteors, asteroids, comets, and . . . and . . .

"Mary-Kate!" Ashley gasped.

"What?" Mary-Kate asked.

"I think I just spotted a UFO!" Ashley said. She squinted through the telescope. "There's a red light right in the middle of the sky! And it's blinking like crazy!"

"You mean an alien spaceship?" Mary-Kate said. She ran over to Ashley. "Now *that's* my kind of astronomy!"

Ashley stood up. She waited while Mary-Kate pressed her eye to the eyepiece.

"Well?" Ashley asked. "Do you see it?"

After a few seconds Mary-Kate heaved a big sigh.

"*That's* not a spaceship," she said. "That's the light on top of the Sears Tower!"

Ashley felt herself blush. "So? The spaceship could have landed on the roof."

"No such luck," Mary-Kate said. She tilted the telescope down to the street.

"Mary-Kate, what are you doing?" Ashley asked.

"Checking our own planet for signs of intelligent life," Mary-Kate said. "Hello, Dearborn Street!"

"Mary-Kate!" Ashley warned. "You remember what Dad said when he gave us this telescope. We're supposed to use it to explore the heavenly bodies!"

"That's exactly what I'm doing!" Mary-Kate said. She adjusted the focus. "I'm exploring Sal Rafanello on his way to wrestling practice!"

"Sal?" Ashley gasped. Sal Rafanello was the cutest high-school hunk on the block. He was also Ashley's crush of the week.

"Give me that thing!" Ashley demanded.

Ashley grabbed the telescope and squinted. She caught a glimpse of Sal just as he was turning the corner. Too late!

Ashley was about to give the telescope back to

4

Mary-Kate, when she saw seventh-grader Bree Montez crossing the street.

"Oh, no!" Ashley gasped. "I can't believe it! It's a crime! It's a felony!"

"What? What?" Mary-Kate cried. She shook Ashley's shoulders. "Do you see a robbery?"

"No," Ashley said. "Worse. Bree Montez is wearing the *exact* same fleece jacket as mine. She knew I bought it at the mall last week. How can she do this to me?"

"Are you sure it's the same jacket?" Mary-Kate asked. "Yours has fuzzy leopard-print buttons."

Ashley steadied the telescope.

"Rats!" she groaned. "I can see two billion light years away with this thing, but I can't see the buttons on a dumb fleece jacket!"

"Bummer." Mary-Kate sighed. Then she snapped her fingers. "Hey—I know! Why don't we start using the power lens? You know, the one that came with the telescope."

"Good idea," Ashley said. "But I can't remember where Dad stashed it."

Mary-Kate pointed to the far side of the attic.

"Most of Dad's junk is behind those boxes. Maybe we'll find the lens back there."

Maybe . . . and maybe we could find a needle in

5

a haystack, too, Ashley thought.

Mary-Kate wiggled behind the tower of boxes. After a few seconds she called out, "Eight-track tapes, a lava lamp, a deflated beanbag chair—wow! It's like discovering a long-lost civilization!"

"Stop fooling around," Ashley said. "Just find the lens!"

"Catch!" Mary-Kate said. She tossed a box out to Ashley.

"Cool!" Ashley said, catching it. She took the lens out and carefully screwed it onto the telescope. "Now we're in business, right, Mary-Kate? . . . Mary-Kate?"

Ashley glanced over her shoulder and sighed. Her sister was still rummaging through their dad's junk!

"Mary-Kate?" Ashley called. "Are you trying on Dad's 'Summer of Love' T-shirt again?"

Mary-Kate let out a whistle. Then she emerged from behind the boxes—carrying a silver saxophone!

Ashley jumped up from her chair. "Wow! I never saw that before. Where did it come from?"

"Maybe it belonged to Mom," Mary-Kate suggested.

Ashley shook her head. She remembered a lot

about their mom, who died three years ago, but she didn't remember a saxophone.

"Maybe it's Dad's," Ashley suggested.

"Dad—a musician?" Mary-Kate laughed. She tossed the saxophone on the sofa. "He sings 'Happy Birthday' off-key!"

"You're right!" Ashley laughed. "Dad's singing is so bad, he can clear a room—"

"Hi, girls!"

Ashley froze. Standing at the attic door, wearing an apron, was their father!

"Um," Ashley said. "Hi, Dad!"

"What's cooking?" Mary-Kate asked.

"Glad you asked," Kevin Burke said. "I've got a cosmic meatloaf with crusty craters in the oven!"

Ashley rolled her eyes. Their science professor dad was taking their astronomy class a little too seriously!

"Gee, Dad," Mary-Kate said. "Sounds . . . out of this world!"

"You girls have been spending a lot of time in the attic lately," Kevin said. He pointed to the telescope. "You haven't been snooping on our neighbors again, have you?"

The twins looked at each other and laughed nervously.

"Snooping?" Mary-Kate asked. "No way!"

"In fact, we were hardly using the telescope at all, Dad," Ashley insisted.

"Yeah!" Mary-Kate blurted. "I was playing the saxophone. And Ashley was—"

"Dancing!" Ashley said. She gave a little twirl.

Kevin stared at the girls. "Did you say . . . saxophone?"

Mary-Kate nodded. She lifted the saxophone from the sofa and held it up. "I found it in your junk pile. It was in a black case covered with dust."

Kevin ran his fingers through his hair. "So that's where I put it," he said softly.

"Dad?" Mary-Kate asked. "That saxophone doesn't belong to you, does it?"

"Me?" Kevin asked in a high voice. He waved his hand. "Um . . . yeah, but I didn't play it very much."

"I'll say!" Ashley said. "It has more dust on it than Mary-Kate's dresser!"

"Cute." Mary-Kate smirked. She held the saxophone out to Kevin. "Here, Dad. Why don't you give it a wail?"

"Please? For old time's sake?" Ashley said.

Kevin took a step back, waving his hands. "N-n-no!"

Ashley stared at her dad. It was just a saxophone.

8

Why was he acting so loopy?

"I just came up to tell you that there's a blue moon tonight," Kevin said. "You might want to check it out."

Mary-Kate and Ashley nodded.

"And while I'm here, I also want to remind you not to snoop." Kevin pointed at the telescope. "Last time I let you girls off easy.

"Next time—watch out!"

CHAPTER TWO

"Boy, was that close!" Ashley said after Kevin left the attic.

Mary-Kate tossed the saxophone back on the sofa. Then she ran over to the telescope.

"I'll say!" Mary-Kate said. "Now, where was I? Maybe I can get the movie theater on Tompkins Street with this thing. Then we can see who's dating who."

"Mary-Kate, are you for real?" Ashley cried. "We just came two inches away from being grounded."

"So?" Mary-Kate shrugged.

"So it's outer space or nothing," Ashley ordered. She pointed to the telescope. "Check out that blue moon!"

"Okay, okay," Mary-Kate said. "But it better be

blue, or I'm checking out Sal's older brother!"

Mary-Kate squinted through the telescope. She pulled her head back and whistled.

"Wow," she said. "This power lens is powerful, all right. I can practically see the Cubs game!"

"Mary-Kate," Ashley said. She folded her arms across her chest. "The moon is in the sky, remember?"

"Yeah, yeah. I remember," she said, focusing the lens. Now she could see all the way down the block to their best friend Max's house.

"Hey!" she said. "Max is sitting on his stoop. He's reading the school paper. Last week's edition. Third page. Wow, this lens is strong!"

"Max is probably reading the sports page again," Ashley said. "What's so interesting about that?"

Mary-Kate peered into the telescope. "Because he's not reading the sports page this time. He's staring at a picture of some girl."

"A girl?" Ashley asked. She walked over to Mary-Kate and leaned over her shoulder. "That's weird. Max couldn't care less about girls."

Mary-Kate looked through the telescope. "That's what *we* thought," she said. "It's a picture of Courtney Russell!"

"Courtney Russell?" Ashley shrieked. "No way!"

11

Mary-Kate nodded. Courtney Russell was the smartest girl in the seventh grade. She was always winning all kinds of awards.

"That picture is from the science fair," Mary-Kate said. "You know, from when she won second prize for growing fungus on a toothbrush."

"Yuck!" Ashley said.

Mary-Kate pressed her eye against the eyepiece. "Ashley! Max is tearing Courtney's picture out of the paper!"

"Maybe he wants to wrap his gum in it," Ashley said.

"I don't think so!" Mary-Kate clutched the telescope. "He's staring at Courtney's picture with a goofy look on his face. The same kind you have when you're talking to a guy you like."

Ashley gave Mary-Kate a shove. "I do not look goofy—"

"Wait!" Mary-Kate interrupted. "Max is folding Courtney's picture in half. Now into fourths. He's sticking it in his pocket!"

"No way!" Ashley cried.

"Yes way! You do know what this means, don't you, Ashley?"

"Are you kidding?" Ashley squealed. "It means Max has a crush on Courtney Russell!"

Mary-Kate and Ashley gave each other a high five. Then Ashley grabbed at the telescope.

"This I've got to see," Ashley said.

"Uh-uh!" Mary-Kate said. She moved the telescope away. "You said you didn't want to snoop, remember?"

"That was before things got juicy!" Ashley declared.

"Mary-Kate! Ashley! The meatloaf is ready. Get it while it's hot!" Kevin called upstairs.

"Okay, Dad!" Mary-Kate yelled back. She tilted the telescope toward the sky.

"What are you doing?" Ashley asked.

"Just in case Dad quizzes us about the blue moon," Mary-Kate said. "I want to be prepared."

She peered through the telescope and frowned. "Dad's got to be kidding," she said. "That moon's not blue."

"Blue moons aren't really blue," Ashley explained patiently. "They're full moons that occur twice in one month. It only happens every two years or so."

"Whatever," Mary-Kate said. She shrugged. "It still looks like a pepperoni pizza with extra cheese. Let's go downstairs."

Mary-Kate dragged the telescope away from the window. She and Ashley had accomplished a lot that evening. They found out that their dad had once played the sax—and they found out that their friend Max was head over heels in love!

The next morning Mary-Kate couldn't wait to ask Max about Courtney Russell. She and Ashley ran down to the kitchen just as Kevin was placing their lunch bags on the counter.

"Meatloaf sandwiches for lunch?" Mary-Kate grumbled. She looked into her lunch bag and made a face. "We had meatloaf for dinner last night."

"Yeah, Dad, give us a break," Ashley said. "Next we'll be having meatloaf muffins for breakfast."

Kevin pointed to the plate of muffins on the kitchen table. "How did you guess?"

Mary-Kate made a face. Their dad was always recycling everything—including their meals!

Kevin laughed. "Just kidding."

While the twins grabbed juice and milk from the refrigerator, Kevin straightened his tie in the reflection of the toaster.

"I have a meeting with the head of the science department tonight," Kevin said. "I'll probably be home late, so I asked Carrie to come over and watch you."

Carrie Moore was one of Kevin's college students. She was also the twins' baby-sitter. Mary-

Kate and Ashley thought they were too old for a sitter until they met Carrie. She wore cool clothes, did fun things, and once even tried to roast marshmallows in the microwave!

Kevin pointed to the refrigerator. "Now, I put a fresh container of saxophone in the fridge—"

Mary-Kate stared at Kevin. What did he just say?

"I mean—a fresh container of milk!" Kevin said quickly. He blushed as he grabbed a piece of toast from the toaster.

"Dad?" Ashley asked. "Are you feeling okay?"

"Sure," Kevin said, sitting down. "Couldn't be better."

Mary-Kate watched her dad spread jelly on his toast. Except it wasn't jelly—it was chunky salsa!

Dad has been acting really weird since we found that saxophone, she thought. *What's going on?*

"I still can't believe you played the sax, Dad," Ashley said. "Saxophones are so cool."

"Too cool!" Mary-Kate joked. "I always thought you were more the harp type, Dad."

"Okay, okay," Kevin said. "Can we please change the subject? Besides, you girls should not have been snooping through my things."

"Snooping?" Ashley gasped.

"We were just looking for the power lens!" Mary-

Kate insisted. "Who cares about your tie-dyed shirts and disco tapes?"

The back door flew open. Their friends Max and Brian walked in carrying their backpacks.

"Hey, guys!" Mary-Kate said.

"Want a muffin?" Ashley asked.

"No, thanks," Brian said. He pointed to Kevin's plate. "I'd rather have toast and salsa—like your dad's eating!"

Kevin stared down at his toast. He made a face and dropped it on his plate.

"Why don't you kids head off to school?" Kevin said quickly. "I've got some work to do . . . in the attic."

"Your dad's acting bizarro this morning," Max said. He sat down at the table.

"Maybe he's in love," Brian suggested.

Ashley laughed. "Dad? In love? No way!"

Mary-Kate leaned over the table. She gave Max a sly look. "But we know *who is!*"

Max grabbed a muffin. He took a bite. "Oh, yeah? Who?"

The twins stood up and surrounded Max.

"You!" Mary-Kate declared.

"Since when do you have a thing for Courtney, Max?" Ashley asked. "Why didn't you tell us?"

Max sputtered muffin crumbs all over the kitchen table.

"What?" Max cried. "What are you talking about?"

"Last night I just happened to be looking through our telescope," Mary-Kate explained. "And I saw you stuffing a picture of Courtney Russell in your pocket."

Ashley gave Max a thumbs-up sign. "Way to go, Max!"

"C-C-Courtney? I don't have a thing for Courtney!" Max stuttered. "I just saved her picture because she's so smart. You know, to inspire me to do my . . . homework."

Brian scratched his chin.

"Come to think of it, Max," he said. "The other day at our softball game you jumped up and started yelling, 'Go, Courtney! Run to third, Courtney! Run to third!'"

"So?" Max demanded.

"The runner's name was Jack!" Brian said.

"Arrgh!" Max cried. He turned to the twins. "You and that dumb telescope!"

"Don't be mad, Max," Ashley said. "It's okay to have a crush on someone."

"Sure it is!" Mary-Kate said. She grinned.

"Ashley has a new one every other day!"

"NOT!" Ashley protested.

"If you want," Mary-Kate offered, "we'll tell you everything we know about girls and dating."

Max jumped up. Brian chased him as he ran out the door.

"Why didn't you tell me, Max?" Brian shouted. "This is serious—it's a major guy thing!"

When the boys were gone, Ashley turned to Mary-Kate.

"Are you happy now, Mary-Kate?" Ashley snapped. "Max is totally embarrassed! I told you we shouldn't have snooped."

Mary-Kate shook her head and smiled.

"Max may be a little mad at us now," she said. "But later on he'll thank us."

"Thank us?" Ashley cried. "For what?"

"For taking an active interest in his love life!" Mary-Kate smiled. "I don't know how——but we've got to help Max with his new girlfriend!"

"Courtney's not his girlfriend."

"No, she's not," Mary-Kate agreed. "Not yet!"

CHAPTER THREE

"Hey, guys," Carrie Moore called as she walked into the house that afternoon. "It's me! Your favorite sitter!"

Carrie spread her arms wide. She waited for an answer. When there was none, she shut the door.

Oh, well, I guess the twins aren't home yet, Carrie thought. She dropped her book bag on the hall table.

Carrie was about to head toward the kitchen when she heard the soft sound of music. It wasn't the twins' usual rock or rap. It was something they never listened to—jazz!

Carrie followed the music up the stairs. It seemed to be coming from the attic. Slowly she opened the attic door. Then she peeked in—and smiled.

Kevin stood in the middle of the attic wearing dark sunglasses. He was playing a saxophone!

Wow! Carrie thought. *I didn't know Professor Burke knew anything about music.*

Kevin was standing with his back to the door. He didn't see Carrie come in. He lowered his sax and smiled coolly. "That was for the very special lady at table three," Kevin said in a deep voice.

"And now, me and the boys will play a little something off our latest CD."

Carrie glanced around. There was no one else in the attic. She smothered a laugh. So Professor Burke wasn't totally grown up after all!

He went through a soft, slow version of "My Favorite Things." This time Carrie couldn't control herself. She began to clap and cheer as he played the last note.

"Bravo!" she cried. "Bravo, Professor Burke!"

Kevin spun around. He honked his sax like a goose.

"Carrie!" he sputtered. "What are you doing here?"

"I work here." Carrie shrugged. "I'm the baby-sitter, remember?"

"I mean up here," Kevin said. "In the attic."

"I followed the music," Carrie explained. "Professor Burke, you're really good. I didn't know you played the sax."

Kevin reddened and looked down at his saxophone.

"Since I was a kid," he said. "Back in college I played in a jazz band."

"No kidding!" Carrie exclaimed. *Why does Professor Burke look embarrassed?* she wondered. *Playing the saxophone is so cool.*

"Mary-Kate found it up here yesterday," Kevin said. "I haven't touched it in years."

Carrie watched as a dreamy look came over Kevin's face.

"Those were the days." He sighed. "We'd rehearse in a dingy little basement."

Carrie spread her arms. "And now you're in the attic. Well, at least you moved up!"

"Very funny," Kevin said. "Actually the acoustics up here are pretty good!"

"And no one will bother you up here, either," Carrie pointed out.

"That's what I thought," Kevin hinted.

"Whoops." Carrie felt herself blush. "So, now that I'm here—will you play something?"

"Not in front of you," Kevin said.

Carrie sighed. "Okay—I get the message. See you!"

She could hear Kevin starting another tune as she slipped out of the attic.

Professor Burke is really good, Carrie thought as she walked down the stairs. *But if he's that good, why is it such a secret?*

Kevin was still playing when the doorbell rang.

"I'll get it!" Carrie called. She ran to the door and opened it. Mrs. Baker, the twins' other sitter, was standing on the stoop.

"Hello, Carrie, dear," Mrs. Baker said.

Carrie smiled at Mrs. Baker. She was wearing her gray hair in a bun. A brown cardigan sweater was buttoned across her flowered housedress.

"Hi, Mrs. Baker," Carrie said. "What's up?"

"My boyfriend, Mr. Fillmore, is trying to take a nap," Mrs. Baker said. "Would you mind asking the professor to put a lid on it?"

Carrie looked at her watch. "Henry's taking a nap now? Doesn't he usually sweep his stoop at three o'clock?"

"Yes, dear," Mrs. Baker said. "But today Henry needs an extra hour of rest. He's flying to Florida tomorrow to visit his evil sister."

Carrie wrinkled her nose. She thought evil sisters lived in fairy tales—not in Miami Beach!

"What is she?" Carrie asked. "Some kind of witch?"

Mrs. Baker nodded. "Warts and all. She visited us last month and didn't approve one bit of our relationship."

"Why not?" Carrie asked.

"She thinks I'm too young for Henry," Mrs. Baker said, patting her gray hair. "He's seventy-four. I'm only seventy-three!"

"I guess you can't blame her," Carrie joked. "You senior citizens can be pretty wild!"

Carrie saw Mary-Kate and Ashley walking up to the stoop. She gave them a little wave.

"Anyway," Mrs. Baker went on, "I can't stand that woman. When I found out that Henry was going to see her, I could have killed him!"

Mary-Kate's eyes widened. "Who's Mr. Fillmore seeing?" she asked. "And why do you want to kill him?"

Mrs. Baker wagged her finger at Mary-Kate.

"Young lady, this is grown-up talk. Don't snoop!"

Mary-Kate and Ashley looked at each other.

"Snoop?" Mary-Kate said.

Ashley grinned. "Who, us?"

CHAPTER FOUR

"Max was pretty quiet in school today," Ashley told Mary-Kate as they walked into the bedroom they shared. "Do you think he'll ever forgive us?"

"He'd better," Mary-Kate said. She looked at the softball trophies lining her shelf. "Or I'll have to find someone else to pitch knuckleballs to!"

Mary-Kate dumped her backpack on the floor. As usual, Ashley placed her backpack neatly on her desk.

"Whew!" Ashley sighed. She rubbed her shoulder. "I don't remember my backpack being so heavy this morning."

"Have you been sneaking makeup to school again?" Mary-Kate demanded.

"No!" Ashley insisted. She unzipped her backpack and looked inside. "Hey, wait a minute. This doesn't belong to me." She pulled a sunflower-print notebook from her backpack.

"Whose is it?" Mary-Kate asked.

Ashley opened the notebook to the first page. "It's Courtney Russell's!" she said.

"You mean, Courtney the Brain?" Mary-Kate asked. "What's her notebook doing in your backpack?"

"Courtney and I have the exact same backpacks," Ashley said. "She must have dropped her notebook in mine by mistake."

"Let me see!" Mary-Kate said. She grabbed the notebook from Ashley and began flipping through it.

"Mary-Kate, what are you doing?" Ashley asked.

"Just seeing if Courtney gets as many A's as we think she does," Mary-Kate explained.

"Oh, no you don't!" Ashley said. She grabbed the notebook back. "Notebooks are too private."

"No, they're not," Mary-Kate argued. "Notebooks are just for study notes and homework assignments. Your basic boring school stuff."

"You don't understand, Mary-Kate," Ashley said. She jabbed at a page in the notebook. "A person's notebook is sacred. It contains more than just tests and homework. It has doodles and telephone numbers and . . . and . . ."

"What?" Mary-Kate urged.

Ashley stared at the page. "Love poems!"

"Love poems!" Mary-Kate repeated. "You've got to be kidding!" She craned her neck to look at the notebook.

"It's a love poem all right," Ashley said. "Listen to this."

Ashley sat down on her pink quilted bedspread. She placed the notebook on her lap and cleared her throat. Then she began to read:

"His eyes are warm and brown . . . his hair as soft as flax . . . there's no one in the world that I love more than—"

Ashley gulped. She blinked a couple of times.

"Than who?" Mary-Kate asked. "Who?"

Ashley looked up from the poem. ". . . than Max!"

The twins stared at each other.

"Did you just say, 'Max'?" Mary-Kate gasped. "I don't believe it!"

Ashley couldn't believe it either. She glanced down at the poem. It did say "Max"—in bright purple ink!

"There's got to be some mistake," Ashley said.

"I'll say!" Mary-Kate said. "Max is cute, but he's not exactly Will Smith."

Ashley couldn't stop shaking her head. "Who would have guessed—Max and Courtney!"

"You mean Stinky and the Brain!" Mary-Kate joked. She plopped down on her own bed. "This is it. This is how we'll help Max!"

"I get it!" Ashley said. "We'll tell him about the poem. He'll stop hating us—and we'll get to help him at the same time. He might even thank us for snooping!"

Ashley reached for the phone on their night table. She hummed a little tune as she pushed in Max's number. The phone rang twice before Max picked up.

"Hello?" he asked.

Ashley put her hand over the phone. "It's Max! It's Max!" she whispered to Mary-Kate.

"Tell him! Tell him!" Mary-Kate whispered back.

"Hi, Max, it's Ashley," Ashley said. She could hardly wait to tell him the good news.

"Don't tell me!" Max said angrily. "You have the telescope pointed at me right now. Wait—so I can pick my nose!"

"Don't be gross, Max!" Ashley snapped. "Mary-Kate and I are not snooping on you. We're just calling with some awesome news."

"Did I win the softball raffle?" Max asked.

"Better!" Ashley said seriously. "Mary-Kate and I found Courtney Russell's notebook. There was a poem inside."

"Oh, so now you're snooping through people's notebooks!" Max said. "How sneaky can you two—"

"It was a love poem, Max!" Ashley interrupted. "A love poem about you!"

There was a long moment of silence.

"Are you sure?" Max asked in a high, squeaky voice.

Ashley recited Courtney's poem line by line. When she was finished, she smiled into the phone.

"Well?" she asked. "What do you think?"

There was another moment of silence. Then Max let out a loud whoop.

"What do I think?" Max shouted. "I'm the man! I'm the man! I'm the man!"

"Ouch!" Ashley pulled the phone away from her ear.

"But what do I do now?" Max asked. "I never had a"—he gulped— "a girlfriend before."

Ashley shivered with excitement. Max actually wanted her advice!

"Pretend that you never heard the poem,"

Ashley said. "Just start doing little things for Courtney to make her know that you like her, too."

"I know!" Max said. "Tomorrow morning I'll pick the raisins out of my bran muffin and give them all to her!"

Ashley rolled her eyes. When it came to romance, Max had a long way to go!

"I don't think so," she said. "Why don't you pick her some flowers instead?"

"Flowers?" Max asked.

"Courtney has a sunflower notebook," Ashley explained. "She even doodled flowers all around her poem. She must have a thing for them!"

"Then flowers it is!" Max said. "Thanks, Ashley. And thank Mary-Kate for me. Bye!"

Ashley heard a click. She hung up the phone and threw her fist into the air.

"Max is our friend again!" Ashley cheered.

"Great!" Mary-Kate said. She grabbed the notebook and began flipping through it again. "Let's see if Courtney has nacho stains on her homework like everyone else."

"No way." Ashley plucked the book from her sister's hands. "We had a one page deal, remember? Besides, we should return Courtney's notebook right away. She's probably wondering where it is."

"Okay," Mary-Kate grumbled.

The twins told Carrie they'd be right back. Then they headed straight for Courtney's house.

"Are you sure this is her house?" Ashley asked Mary-Kate as they walked up Buckingham Street.

Mary-Kate compared the address on Courtney's notebook to the address on the corner brownstone.

"This is the place," Mary-Kate said with a nod.

They were about to walk up the front steps to the red town house when the door opened. Courtney Russell walked out. She was wearing black stretch pants, a white T-shirt, and a gray sweater.

"Hi, Courtney!" Mary-Kate called.

Courtney looked surprised to see the twins. "Hi, Mary-Kate. Hi, Ashley," she said.

"Guess what!" Ashley said. She held up her notebook and smiled. "This was in my backpack."

Courtney's brown eyes lit up. "My notebook!" she sighed with relief. "I was so worried that I lost it. I promised Miss Tandy that I'd hand in a poem for extra credit tomorrow."

Ashley gave Mary-Kate a sly look. "Poem?" Ashley repeated.

"What kind of poem?" Mary-Kate asked coolly.

"My poem about Max!" Courtney said. "But I want to change it just a bit."

Ashley glanced at Mary-Kate from the corner of her eye. This was getting good. Very good!

"How are you going to change it?" Mary-Kate asked.

Courtney's eyes twinkled. "I want to write all about Max's big fluffy tail!"

Ashley stared at Courtney. Did she say—?

"Big . . . fluffy . . . tail?" Ashley gulped.

The door of the house swung open and a brown and white dog ran out. He panted as he raced down the stoop. When he reached the sidewalk, he jumped up on Mary-Kate.

"Hey!" Mary-Kate said. She fell back on the sidewalk as the big dog licked her face.

"Down, boy!" Courtney scolded. "Down, Max!"

Mary-Kate looked up at the slobbering dog. "Courtney?" she asked. "Did you just call that dog . . . Max?"

"Yes!" Courtney said. She grabbed Max's collar and pulled him off of Mary-Kate. "He's our new puppy. Isn't he great?"

Ashley pointed to the dog. "S-s-so the poem you wrote was about—"

"My dog, Max!" Courtney declared proudly.

"Oh, boy," Ashley muttered under her breath. She and Mary-Kate would have to warn Max—

before he ran into Courtney.

But when Ashley glanced up the block she saw something that made her stomach flip.

It was Max. He was walking toward them with a grin on his face—and flowers in his hand!

CHAPTER FIVE

"It's Max!" Ashley said quickly. She looked down at the dog. "The other Max!"

Mary-Kate was desperate. She tried throwing Max a signal that they used during softball—the signal that told a runner to stay at the base!

"Mary-Kate?" Courtney asked. "Is something wrong?"

Mary-Kate waved her arms in the air. But it was too late.

Max walked over to Courtney and held out the flowers.

"My mom said I couldn't pick from our garden," Max said. "So I hope you like plastic."

"Um," Ashley said. She grabbed Max's arm.

"Courtney is allergic to plastic!"

"No, I'm not," Courtney said.

"Then, we're late for softball practice," Mary-Kate blurted.

"We don't have softball practice today," Max said, smiling at Courtney. "Besides, I thought Courtney and I could hang out."

Courtney stared at the flowers. Then she looked at Mary-Kate, Ashley, and Max.

"Can someone tell me what's going on here?" Courtney said.

Mary-Kate took a deep breath. Then she began to speak.

"We opened your notebook, Courtney," Mary-Kate explained. "And we found the poem you wrote. The one about Max."

"We didn't know it was about your dog," Ashley said.

Mary-Kate could hear Max drop the flowers on the sidewalk with a clunk.

"Dog?" he cried. "You mean she was writing about a stupid mutt?"

"Max is not a mutt!" Courtney declared. "And he's not stupid!"

Max the dog wagged his tail.

"We're sorry, Max," Ashley told her friend.

"We were just trying to help."

"And we know you like Courtney!" Mary-Kate said. She saw Max hit his forehead. "I mean—because she's so intelligent!"

"Arrgh!" Max groaned. He turned to Mary-Kate and Ashley. "I should never have trusted your snooping!"

"But, Max—" Mary-Kate started to say.

Max whirled around and stomped up the block. When he turned the corner, Mary-Kate looked at Courtney. She was about to apologize when Courtney began to giggle.

"This is too funny!" Courtney said. "Max thought that I was in love with him! Wait until I tell my friends!"

Ashley's eyes widened in horror. "No, Courtney, don't—"

Courtney waved to two girls across the street.

"Lynn, Keisha!" she called. "Wait up! I've got something to tell you!"

Mary-Kate watched Courtney run across the street. Then she looked down at the dog.

"Why couldn't your name be Buster or Tramp?" she moaned. "Why did it have to be Max?"

The dog lowered his head and whined. Then he trotted up the steps and into the house.

Ashley planted her hands on her hips.

"Well, Mary-Kate?" she snapped. "Are you happy now?"

"Me?" Mary-Kate cried. "You were the one who told Max about the poem!"

"But it was your idea to snoop," Ashley insisted.

"It was your backpack!" Mary-Kate exclaimed.

The twins plopped down on Courtney's stoop. They leaned forward and rested their chins in their hands.

"Mary-Kate?" Ashley said. "I think it's time to make a pact."

"The last pact we made was to stop biting our nails," Mary-Kate muttered. "What is it this time?"

"Never to snoop again!" Ashley said firmly.

"Never?" Mary-Kate cried.

Ashley nodded. "You saw the trouble it got us into. Not to mention what it did to Max."

"Okay," Mary-Kate said, sighing. "No more snooping."

CHAPTER SIX

"What should we do now?" Mary-Kate asked as she and Ashley walked up to the attic.

"Well, we can always do homework," Ashley suggested.

"Homework—now, there's a concept," Mary-Kate grumbled. "What do we have today?"

"Math, social studies," Ashley listed. "Astronomy—"

"Astronomy, huh?" Mary-Kate said. "At least the telescope is still good for something."

The twins entered the attic. They stood six feet away from the telescope and stared at it with longing.

"Maybe we can lock it in the 'solar system' position," Mary-Kate suggested.

"Yeah," Ashley said. "There's nobody to snoop on in outer space."

"Except hunky aliens," Mary-Kate joked.

Ashley leaned on the telescope as she looked out of the window. She could see the lights on in Mrs. Baker's house across the street. Mrs. Baker and Mr. Fillmore were standing in front of the living room window.

"It's date night at Mrs. Baker's," Ashley sighed. "I don't need a telescope to tell me that."

Ashley was about to turn away when she saw something else. Mr. Fillmore was waving two pointy objects at Mrs. Baker. They looked like knitting needles.

"Hey," Ashley said. "There's something going on at Mrs. Baker's house. Check it out."

Mary-Kate squinted her eyes and peered out the window. "It looks like Mrs. Baker and Mr. Fillmore are having a fight!" she said, and grabbed the telescope.

Ashley stared at Mary-Kate. Was her sister nuts?

"Mary-Kate!" Ashley cried. "We just made a pact not to snoop, remember?"

"This is different," Mary-Kate said, adjusting the focus. "Mrs. Baker could be in danger. I'm just being a good neighbor."

"Go ahead," Ashley said. She paced the attic nervously. "You can snoop if you want to. But we made a pact, and I'm sticking with it."

"Suit yourself," Mary-Kate said. "But Mrs. Baker has just picked up a huge knife!"

"A knife?" Ashley shrieked. She shoved Mary-Kate off the chair. "Give me that thing!"

Ashley pressed her eye against the telescope. Sure enough, Mrs. Baker was waving a knife at Mr. Fillmore!

"Wow!" she said. "I wonder why they're fighting."

"I'll bet it's because of that other woman Mrs. Baker was talking about. Mr. Fillmore must be seeing her, too!" Mary-Kate declared.

"But he's so old!" Ashley exclaimed. "How does he have the energy to date two people at the same time?"

"Let me see again," Mary-Kate said. She took the telescope from Ashley and steadied it.

"Mrs. Baker is pulling down the shade," Mary-Kate said in a hushed voice. "But I can still see her shadow."

Suddenly she gasped. "Ashley! She's raising her knife in the air! Oh, no! Mr. Fillmore has disappeared!"

Mary-Kate spun around and stared at Ashley. "His shadow has slipped right off the shade! Do you know what that means?"

"No, what?" Ashley asked.

"I think Mr. Fillmore is gone for good," Mary-Kate said slowly. "I think Mrs. Baker's killed him!"

Ashley stared at her sister.

"You're losing it, Mary-Kate," Ashley said. "Mrs. Baker is not a cold-blooded murderer. There's got to be an explanation."

"Think about it, Ashley," Mary-Kate said. "Mr. Fillmore is dating another woman, right? And Mrs. Baker said it made her so mad that she could kill him!"

"It's just an expression," Ashley said. "Besides, Mrs. Baker couldn't stab Mr. Fillmore!"

"Why not?" Mary-Kate asked.

"Because she has arthritis!" Ashley insisted. "She can't even slice a pound cake!"

Mary-Kate paced the attic. "We have to blow the whistle on Mrs. Baker," she said. "We have to tell Dad."

"Dad?" Ashley shrieked. "If he finds out we were snooping again, he'll freak."

"He'll freak if he finds out we saw a crime committed and didn't tell him," Mary-Kate said.

Ashley rolled her eyes. There was no talking Mary-Kate out of this one!

"Dad won't be home until late tonight," Ashley pointed out. "He said he has a meeting, remember?"

"Then we'll tell Carrie instead," Mary-Kate said. "Someone has to know."

"Know what?" Carrie asked. She poked her head through the attic door.

Ashley gulped. "Mary-Kate thinks—"

"I think I saw Mrs. Baker kill Mr. Fillmore," Mary-Kate interrupted. She described the scene in Mrs. Baker's house.

Carrie stared in disbelief. "Mrs. Baker wouldn't hurt a fly," she said. She began to laugh. "That's one of the silliest ideas I've ever heard!"

"But Carrie, could you at least talk to Mrs. Baker and make sure?" Mary-Kate asked.

"Mrs. Baker has enough on her mind without having to defend herself against murder charges!" Carrie snorted.

"Now, come on down and get some dinner." She pointed to the window. "And stay away from that telescope!"

"Now are you satisfied?" Ashley asked when Carrie had gone.

"I'm still going to tell Dad," Mary-Kate insisted.

"I'll stay up all night if I have to—until he comes home!"

"Fine!" Ashley said. "But you're obviously totally wrong about Mrs. Baker."

Mary-Kate stared out the window. "I hope you're right, Ashley. But I know what I saw—and it doesn't look good."

CHAPTER SEVEN

"Mary-Kate," Ashley mumbled later that night. She rolled over in her bed. "Turn off the light. I want to go to sleep."

Mary-Kate sat up in her own bed. She stared over at her sister.

"Sleep?" Mary-Kate cried. "You said you were going to stay awake until Dad got home. So we can both tell him about Mrs. Baker!"

"*You* wanted to tell him about Mrs. Baker, not me," Ashley said. "Besides, I didn't think I'd be this tired."

"Great," Mary-Kate muttered. "We have a crime to report and you're sleeping on the job. Some partner!"

Ashley snuggled under her pink quilt. "Mmm-hmmm."

"What if Mrs. Baker is on her way over here right now?" Mary-Kate whispered. "What if she saw us snooping and now she wants to—"

A dark shadow loomed across the doorway. Mary-Kate grabbed her pillow and clutched it.

"W-who's there?" Mary-Kate stuttered.

Carrie appeared at the door.

"You were expecting the tooth fairy?" Carrie joked. She pointed to Mary-Kate's nightstand. "What's with the light, Mary-Kate? I promised your dad you'd be asleep by the time he got back."

Mary-Kate bolted up in bed.

"I was just—reading!" she said quickly.

"Really?" Carrie asked. "What are you reading? Anything good?"

Mary-Kate grabbed a book from her nightstand. She looked at the cover and jumped. It was a murder mystery!

"Ahh!" Mary-Kate shrieked. She reached over and tossed the book under her bed.

Carrie stared at Mary-Kate. "Mary-Kate? Is something wrong?"

"No. I-I just thought I saw a spider," Mary-Kate said.

"Well, let me know if you see any more," Carrie said. "We don't want an invasion."

As Carrie left the room, Mary-Kate called out to her, "Will Dad be home soon?"

"He'd better be," Carrie sighed. "I read my biology chapter three times. I also saw a movie on TV."

"What was it?" Mary-Kate asked.

"*Nightmare on Elm Street*," Carrie said.

Mary-Kate gulped as Carrie closed the door.

"Good night, you guys," Carrie said. "And turn off the light right now."

"Good night," Ashley yawned.

Mary-Kate switched off the light. The room was dark and quiet. The tree branches outside the shade looked like a bony, clutching claw.

"I wonder what Mrs. Baker did with Mr. Fillmore's body," Mary-Kate whispered. "Ashley? Ashley?"

Mary-Kate looked over at Ashley's bed. Her sister was already fast asleep.

Look at her, Mary-Kate thought. *Completely out. Snoring, too. Well, I'm staying awake.*

Mary-Kate's eyelids began to feel heavy. She leaned back on her pillow and yawned.

I can't fall asleep, Mary-Kate thought. *Not when Mrs. Baker is a baker . . . I mean a murderer. . . .*

Mary-Kate pulled her quilt up to her chin.

I'll just take a little nap, Mary-Kate thought. *There's nothing wrong with a power snooze. This way I'll be fresh and alert when Dad . . . comes . . . home. . . .*

"Mary-Kate? Mary-Kate?" Ashley asked. She shook Mary-Kate awake. "Did you speak to Dad last night?"

"Huh?" Mary-Kate asked. She looked up from her pillow. Ashley was standing next to her bed.

"About Mrs. Baker?" Ashley asked.

Mary-Kate bolted upright. She looked at the clock. She had fallen asleep before Kevin came home. And she slept the whole night through!

"No," Mary-Kate said. She hopped out of bed. "But I will right now!"

"Mary-Kate, Ashley!" Kevin called from downstairs. "You're going to be late for school if you don't get ready!"

The twins quickly washed and got dressed. They ran downstairs to the kitchen.

"Good morning," Kevin said. He was cutting tuna sandwiches in half. "I overslept by fifteen minutes. So you'd better shake a leg!"

Ashley sat down at the breakfast table. But Mary-Kate followed Kevin around the kitchen.

"Dad?" she said. "There's something I have to talk to you about."

"Oh?" Kevin said. He began wrapping the sandwiches in cellophane. "Is it about school?"

"Not really," Mary-Kate said. "It's about Mrs. Baker."

"What about her?" Kevin asked. He stuffed the sandwiches in the twins' lunch bags.

Mary-Kate took a deep breath. "Yesterday I saw Mr. Fillmore inside Mrs. Baker's house. The two were—"

"On a date?" Kevin said. He smiled and nodded. "I know it's hard for you to believe, Mary-Kate, but older people like to have fun, too."

"No, Dad," Mary-Kate said. She shook her head. "You see, Mrs. Baker was holding—"

"Mr. Fillmore's hand?" Kevin asked. He began wiping the counter. "I think that's kind of sweet, don't you?"

Mary-Kate formed a T with her hands. "Time out, Dad!" Mary-Kate said. "Mrs. Baker and Mr. Fillmore were doing more than holding hands. They were—"

"Stop right there," Kevin ordered. "I do not want to hear it."

"Why not?" Mary-Kate asked.

"Because it's none of our business," Kevin said.

"Besides, didn't I warn you about snooping?"

"Yeah, but—"

"Now, eat your breakfast, Mary-Kate, or it'll get cold," Kevin said.

"It's cornflakes, Dad," Mary-Kate mumbled.

Kevin didn't answer. He looked at the clock.

"Whoops. Almost forgot," he said. "Classes are canceled today. I have to call Eddie to come over for the broken dishwasher. I'll be right back."

As Kevin ran out of the kitchen, Mary-Kate slumped down at the table.

"So why didn't you tell him?" Ashley asked.

"Because he didn't give me a chance!" Mary-Kate exclaimed. "Besides, he snuck in that little warning about snooping again."

"It's just as well, Mary-Kate," Ashley said. "First of all, the whole idea is ridiculous. Then, second, even if Mrs. Baker did do it, how would we prove it?"

"What do you mean?" Mary-Kate asked.

Ashley shrugged. "We have no evidence!"

Mary-Kate's hand stopped as she reached for the milk. "Ashley, that's it!" she said. "That's what we're going to do right after school today!"

"What?" Ashley asked.

Mary-Kate smiled.

"We're going to look for evidence!"

CHAPTER EIGHT

"So, what's wrong with the dishwasher?" Kevin's friend Eddie asked later that day.

Eddie had been Kevin's friend since college. He was also a handy plumber!

"Every time it drains, water comes shooting up into the sink," Kevin explained. "Isn't there supposed to be one of those metal thingamajigs?"

"Thingamajigs! Cute." Eddie laughed. He crawled under the sink to check the pipes.

Kevin glanced at the clock. He had lots of work to do that day.

"Will this take long, Eddie?" Kevin asked. "I've got to grade some exams on gravity this afternoon."

"Gravity, huh?" Eddie said. His voice echoed

from beneath the sink. "You teach that stuff, too?"

"Yeah—gravity is amazing!" Kevin said excitedly. "Imagine a tremendous force pulling everything toward the center of the earth."

"Like a hair clog," Eddie said.

Kevin raised an eyebrow. "A . . . hair clog?"

"Sure." Eddie stood up from under the sink. "You got stuff like hair, toothpaste, soap gunk—all clumping together in the middle of the pipe. It's a beautiful thing."

"Hi, Professor," a voice called out. The back door opened, and Carrie walked in carrying her book bag. She was wearing a blue minidress and platform boots.

"Oh. Hi, Eddie," she said.

Kevin looked at the clock again. Carrie never came in the middle of the day when the twins were still in school.

"Carrie, what are you doing here?" he said.

"I couldn't wait to tell you the greatest news!" Carrie said.

"Oh, no," Kevin groaned. "You didn't buy that iguana for the twins—"

"No!" Carrie said with a laugh. "On my way home from baby-sitting last night, I stopped off at this jazz club. It's a cool place. They were letting people play along with the band."

Kevin gulped. He had a feeling he knew what Carrie was going to say next.

"It would be the perfect place for you to play your sax, Professor!" Carrie went on.

"Thanks," Kevin said quickly. "But I don't perform anymore."

"But when we were talking in the attic," Carrie said, "it sounded like you really missed it. And for the first time in months you looked like you were having fun!"

"Save your breath, Carrie," Eddie said. He crawled out from under the sink. "Kevin hasn't played in public since Frightful Friday."

Kevin shot Eddie a warning look. Frightful Friday was one night he didn't want to remember!

"Frightful Friday?" Carrie asked. "What was that?"

"Eddie?" Kevin said. He pointed to the sink. "Don't you have a pipe to fix?"

Eddie turned his back to Kevin.

"It was back when Kevin was in college," Eddie explained to Carrie. "He was supposed to play his first gig with a jazz band."

"Really?" Carrie asked. "Go on!"

"The band's onstage and they're cooking!" Eddie

51

waved his wrench in the air. "The piano takes a solo! The trumpet takes a solo! And then it's Kevin's turn to take a solo."

"And we all lived happily ever after." Kevin tried to push Eddie out the door. "Thanks for stopping by, Eddie."

"Wait, Professor Burke," Carrie said. "What happened to your solo?"

Kevin didn't answer. He wished he could jump into the sink and dive down the clogged drain!

"Nothing happened—that's the point," Eddie explained. "Kevin huffed and puffed and couldn't get a note out. He was so embarrassed that he ran off the stage. And he's never played in public since."

"Oh," Carrie said, clicking her tongue. "That is such a sad story."

Kevin glared at his friend. He didn't want anyone to know about the night he made a fool of himself. How could Eddie do this to him?

"Okay," Kevin told Carrie. "So I have a little stage fright."

"You? Stage fright?" Carrie asked. "But you lecture to hundreds of students every day!"

"Yes, but they don't heckle me!" Kevin said.

"Want to bet?" Carrie joked.

Kevin frowned. "Carrie—"

"Fine," Carrie said. "I won't ask you to play your sax in public. But you still listen in public, don't you?"

"Sure." Kevin shrugged. "I love jazz clubs."

"Then come with me to this club tonight," Carrie suggested. "We'll just be two jazz lovers listening to music."

Kevin paused. *Carrie's right*, he thought. *It couldn't really hurt just to listen.*

"All right," Kevin agreed. "I'll come."

"Way to go, Professor!" Carrie said.

Eddie pulled a can of root beer from the refrigerator and popped it open. "I like jazz, too!"

Kevin and Carrie stared at him.

"No," they said at the same time.

"Okay, okay." Eddie put down his root beer and returned to the sink. "I can take a hint."

Kevin smiled at Carrie. Listening to live jazz music would be fun.

As long as he wasn't the one who was playing!

CHAPTER NINE

"Give it up, Mary-Kate," Ashley pleaded.

Mary-Kate had dragged Ashley to Mr. Fillmore's house the second she got out of after-school baseball practice. Now she was banging on his door. She listened with her ear pressed against the door for a moment. Then she knocked again.

"Mr. Fillmore isn't answering," Mary-Kate said. "I'm telling you, Ashley—he's history!"

Ashley stared at the door. Mary-Kate was starting to make her wonder. Was it really possible that something happened to Mr. Fillmore?

No way, she told herself. *This isn't the movies!*

"Mr. Fillmore could be anywhere!" Ashley insisted.

"Sure," Mary-Kate said. "Under the basement, in a trunk—"

Ashley clapped her hands over her ears. "Mary-Kate!"

The twins turned away from Mr. Fillmore's house. They were about to head home when Ashley spotted Mrs. Baker. She was leaving her house with a large plastic bag. Draped over her shoulders was a man's coat.

"There's the suspect now," Ashley joked. "Maybe she'll confess if you rough her up."

"Very funny," Mary-Kate said.

Mary-Kate and Ashley walked over to Mrs. Baker.

"Hey, Mrs. Baker," Mary-Kate said. "What's with the coat? Isn't that Mr. Fillmore's?"

"Yes, it is," Mrs. Baker patted the coat. "But don't worry. He won't be needing it where he's going."

Ashley stared at Mr. Fillmore's coat. Then at the plastic bag.

It was big and bulky. Big enough for a—?

Mrs. Baker dropped the bag just as a garbage truck pulled up to the curb.

"This is heavy," the garbageman grunted as he lifted the bag. "What do you have in here, anyway?"

Mrs. Baker tapped the man's arm and laughed.

"Oh, I'm just getting rid of some old things I don't need anymore," Mrs. Baker explained.

Mary-Kate elbowed Ashley in the ribs.

Old things? Ashley thought. *As in—Mr. Fillmore?*

Ashley gave a little gasp. Maybe Mary-Kate was right. Maybe Mrs. Baker did do away with Mr. Fillmore!

"Really, Mrs. Baker," Mary-Kate asked. "What do you have in that bag?"

"My," Mrs. Baker said, looking down at Mary-Kate. "You're just full of questions, aren't you? Remember, dear. Curiosity killed the cat!"

Killed? Ashley grabbed her sister's arm.

"Uh, we have to go now, Mrs. Baker," she stammered. "S-see you later."

Ashley and Mary-Kate walked quickly back toward their house. When they were finally inside, Mary-Kate slammed the door.

"Mr. Fillmore is halfway to the city dump!" Mary-Kate said. "Now do you believe me?"

"Okay, Mary-Kate. You win," Ashley said, out of breath. "Something is definitely going on."

"Good!" Mary-Kate said. She started walking toward the den. "Then let's tell Dad."

Ding-dong!

"I hope that's Carrie," Ashley said. "Now maybe she'll believe us, too."

Mary-Kate flung the door open. But Carrie wasn't there. Instead, standing on the stoop was—

"Mrs. Baker!" Ashley gasped.

"Hello, girls," Mrs. Baker said. She walked past Ashley and Mary-Kate.

"W-w-what are you doing here?" Mary-Kate stammered.

"What am I doing here?" Mrs. Baker asked with a chuckle. "Why—I'm here to take care of you!"

I knew it! Mary-Kate thought. *Mrs. Baker is going to take care of us, all right—by making us disappear like Mr. Fillmore!*

"Hi, Mrs. Baker," Kevin said, coming into the room. "Ready for a fun-filled night of baby-sitting?"

Mary-Kate turned to her father. "Mrs. Baker—baby-sitting?" she said. "Where's Carrie?"

"Yeah, Dad," Ashley asked. "Where's Carrie?"

"Girls, I'm sorry," Kevin said. "I forgot to tell you. Carrie is taking me to a jazz club tonight."

Mary-Kate's heart sank. She had to think quickly. This was an emergency!

"Great!" she exclaimed. "We'll come, too! We want to hear you play that saxophone."

"Hey!" Kevin objected. "I'm not the one who's

going to be playing! It's going to be—"

"Yeah, let us come!" Ashley said, interrupting him. She wiggled her hips and twirled her finger. "We love to jump, jive, and wail—"

"No can do," Kevin shook his head. "Mrs. Baker is going to watch you and that's that. So behave yourselves."

Mrs. Baker smiled at the twins.

"Oh, they will," she said sweetly.

A car outside honked three times.

"That's Carrie!" Kevin said. "Gotta go!"

Mary-Kate and Ashley tugged at Kevin's arms.

"Wait, Dad!" Ashley begged. "You can't go yet!"

"But we'll be late for the show," Kevin said.

Now Mary-Kate was desperate. "We have to tell you something, Dad," she said. "And it's very important!"

Kevin grinned. "Girls. I know all about the *South Park* TV special tonight. And you can't watch it."

Ashley jumped up and down. "But, Dad—"

"Bye-bye!" Kevin said, slipping out the door.

"Have a good time, Professor Burke," Mrs. Baker called. She closed the door and muttered, "If you like that sort of racket."

Mary-Kate watched as Mrs. Baker locked the door. She could feel her blood turn to ice.

"I'm sorry about *South Park*, girls," Mrs. Baker said. "But we can watch reruns of my favorite show instead."

"Your favorite show?" Mary-Kate asked.

"What's that?" Ashley asked.

Mrs. Baker rubbed her hands together.

"Murder, She Wrote!" she said with a grin.

Mary-Kate looked at Ashley. She knew her sister was thinking the same thing she was.

They were trapped in the house with Mrs. Baker. And there was no way out!

CHAPTER TEN

"I'm sure the twins will be just fine with Mrs. Baker," Carrie said as she drove through the streets of Chicago.

"It's not the twins I'm worried about," Kevin joked. "It's Mrs. Baker!"

Carrie laughed. When she stopped for a red light she turned to Kevin.

"I still can't believe that we both like the same music," she said.

Kevin glanced around Carrie's car. It was about twenty years old. The cracked upholstery was held together with silver tape. There was a furry steering wheel cover and a plastic chihuahua on the dashboard.

"And I can't believe you've been driving my girls around in this thing!" Kevin said. He watched the chihuahua's head bob up and down.

"Don't worry, Professor," Carrie said, patting the steering wheel. "This car is as safe as a tank!"

"It does look pretty solid," Kevin said. He reached out and gave the dashboard a whack.

His seat fell back and collapsed on the floor!

Carrie cleared her throat. "I've been meaning to get that fixed," she said.

Kevin returned his seat to the upright position. He was getting a funny feeling they should have taken the bus. "So," he said, careful not to lean forward again. "Tell me who's playing tonight."

"Well," Carrie said. "I know one guy who's going to play. I've only heard him once, but he was great."

"Oh?" Kevin asked. "Who is it?"

"You!" Carrie said.

Kevin stared at Carrie. She was joking . . . wasn't she?

"No, really," Kevin tried again. "Who is it?"

Kevin could see Carrie grip the steering wheel tightly.

"Look," Carrie said slowly. "I have a confession to make. I kind of tricked you into coming tonight."

"Tricked me?" Kevin asked. "Why?"

"I was hoping that once you got there," Carrie said, "you'd get into the mood and forget all about your fear."

"Stop the car!" Kevin demanded.

"Oh, come on, Professor," Carrie pleaded.

"I said, stop the car!" Kevin insisted.

"Okay," Carrie said. "But it won't do you any good."

The car lurched to a stop. The chihuahua fell into Kevin's lap.

"Thank you," Kevin said. He turned to open the door—but the handle came off in his hand.

"Whoops," Carrie said. "That's something else I've got to fix."

Kevin looked around the car for an escape. He was trapped!

"I'd like to go home!" Kevin said.

"Fine," Carrie said. "But I can't believe you'd give up the fun of playing with a band because of something that happened fifteen years ago!"

"I can't help it if I have stage fright!" Kevin said. "What if I make a fool of myself again?"

Carrie put her hands on the fuzzy steering wheel.

"Okay, I'll turn the car around," she said. "But let

me ask you this: If Mary-Kate blew a basketball throw, or if Ashley tripped in a ballet recital, would you let them quit?"

"Absolutely," he declared. "I'd tell them to walk away and never look back."

Carrie grinned. "You would not!"

"Okay," Kevin said. He sighed. "I'd tell them you can't quit something you love because you messed up once. "

"Then, don't you think it's time for you to give it another shot?" Carrie asked.

Kevin began to feel nervous. Then he thought of a great argument.

"Even if I wanted to play, I couldn't," he said. "I don't have my sax."

He folded his arms triumphantly. *That takes care of that!* he thought.

"It's in the trunk," Carrie said.

"I'd, uh, I'd still need my reeds," Kevin pointed out.

"I bought you a whole new box," Carrie said. "It's in the glove compartment."

Kevin couldn't help smiling. Carrie was one-of-a-kind! "You really thought this out, didn't you?" he asked.

Carrie pulled a pair of black sunglasses from her

pocket. She handed them to Kevin.

"You bet I did," she said.

Kevin put the glasses on. "Maybe I could play just one song . . ." he said dreamily.

As Carrie continued to drive, Kevin gazed out the window. After a while the scenery began to look familiar.

"Carrie?" Kevin asked, lowering his sunglasses. "Didn't we just drive by that burnt-out doughnut shop? About four times?"

Carrie slowed down the car.

"Okay," she sighed. "We're lost. I can't remember how to get to the club. I've only been there once."

"No problem," Kevin said. He started to roll down the window. "We'll just ask for directions."

"Great plan," Carrie said. "Except for one thing."

"What?" Kevin asked.

The car began to hiss and sputter.

"We're out of gas!"

CHAPTER ELEVEN

"Remember," Mary-Kate whispered to Ashley. "One wrong move and it's over for both of us."

"Shh!" Ashley warned. She was so nervous she could feel her heart pounding. "She might hear you."

The twins sat on the sofa in the living room, stiff as boards. Mrs. Baker looked up from the horror book she was reading.

"You girls are awfully quiet this evening," she said.

"We're always quiet!" Mary-Kate said quickly. "You don't have to worry about us talking. To anybody."

"All right, Ashley," Mrs. Baker said.

"I'm Mary-Kate," Mary-Kate corrected. "But

that's okay—you can call me Ashley. You can call me whatever you want!"

Mrs. Baker rose slowly from her chair.

"Well, then," Mrs. Baker said. "How about if I bake some of my killer brownies?"

"K-killer brownies?" Ashley stammered. What if Mrs. Baker's recipe called for a dash of . . . poison?

"No!" Ashley blurted out.

Mary-Kate nudged Ashley hard. "She means . . . no, thank you, Mrs. Baker."

"Then I'll just whip up something else," Mrs. Baker said. She dropped her book on the chair and walked out of the living room.

"Don't eat or drink anything that she brings you!" Mary-Kate whispered.

"Du-uh!" Ashley shot back. Then she grew serious. "What do we do now?"

Mary-Kate jumped up from the sofa. She began to pace back and forth.

"I know!" Mary-Kate said. "I'll sneak over to Mrs. Baker's house and look for evidence."

"And leave me alone with Grandma Slice-and-Dice?" Ashley gasped.

Mary-Kate headed for the door. "I'm going to get to the bottom of this if it kills me!" she said. "I mean—if it's the last thing I do! I mean—if—"

"Mary-Kate, stop!" Ashley called.

But Mary-Kate slipped out the door.

Now Ashley was all alone in the house with Mrs. Baker!

Okay, Ashley thought nervously. *I just have to make sure Mrs. Baker doesn't realize Mary-Kate is gone. Then everything will be fine.*

Ashley pressed her forehead as she paced the living room. Suddenly she had an idea. If they could fool Mrs. Baker by looking alike, maybe they could fool Mrs. Baker by sounding alike, too!

Cupping her hands over her mouth, Ashley shouted toward the kitchen door. "Ashley! I'm going to go upstairs and study!"

Ashley counted to five. Then she shouted again.

"Okay, Mary-Kate! I'll stay down here and watch TV with nice, sweet Mrs. Baker!"

Ashley ran to the sofa and sat down. She clutched a pillow in fear. What if her trick didn't work? What if Mrs. Baker was on to her?

"Ashley! Mary-Kate!" Mrs. Baker called from the kitchen. "I'm just going to step over to my house to get my knitting."

Her house? Ashley panicked. *Mrs. Baker can't go back to her house. Not while Mary-Kate is there!*

"No!" Ashley shouted. She ran to the kitchen just

as Mrs. Baker was pulling on her sweater.

"No! No! No!" Ashley begged, tugging at Mrs. Baker's sleeve.

"Is something wrong, dear?" Mrs. Baker asked.

"No—um," Ashley said, her voice cracking. "I just thought you might like . . . some company."

Mrs. Baker buttoned her sweater and smiled. "Well, isn't that sweet, Mary-Kate!"

"I'm Ashley," Ashley said. "Mary-Kate is upstairs in the attic! Studying! Remember?"

Ashley turned toward the door and shouted, "Mary-Kate! We'll be right back! Don't study too hard!"

Mrs. Baker tapped her ear. "Ashley, dear. You're making my hearing aid screech."

"Sorry," Ashley said.

"Now, come along," Mrs. Baker said. "And put on a jacket, or you'll catch your death of cold."

CHAPTER TWELVE

"Are you sure you called the tow truck?" Kevin asked Carrie. He rested his saxophone on his hip. They had been waiting in the parking lot for what seemed like hours!

"Sure, Professor," Carrie said. She pointed to the bright glow of headlights. "In fact, here it comes now!"

A yellow truck pulled into the parking lot. Kevin watched as a college-age guy jumped out. The name "Frank" was stitched on the front of his coveralls.

"Yo, I'm Frankie!" he said, pointing to Carrie's car. "Is that the clunker—I mean car—that needs towing?"

"That's the one," Kevin said.

Frank grinned when he saw the saxophone in Kevin's hand. "Hey, I love jazz. Do you play that thing?"

Kevin sighed. "Not really, I—"

"Does he play?" Carrie cried. She turned to Kevin. "Go ahead, Professor. You said you'd play for an audience tonight!"

"Yes, but in a jazz club," Kevin argued. "Not a parking lot. And I haven't played for a live audience in fifteen years. I'm still nervous!"

Carrie patted Kevin's shoulder. "Take your time, Professor," she said gently. "Just start playing when the feeling is absolutely right."

"Yeah?" Kevin asked, staring down at the saxophone.

"Sure," Frank agreed. "But just remember, I charge by the minute."

"The minute?" Carrie shrieked. She began jumping up and down. "Professor! What are you waiting for? Start playing already!"

"Okay, okay," Kevin said. He placed the reed to his lips. Then he played the first note. Then another. And another. Until he was playing an entire song!

"Way to go, Professor!" Carrie cheered.

Kevin felt great. *I'm doing it!* he thought.

"Hey," Frank said. "That guy isn't bad."

"Thanks," Carrie said. "I found him in the attic."

"The Attic, huh?" Frank said. "I never heard of that place."

"It's right above the bathroom," Carrie said.

"That place I know!" Frank said. He held a tattooed hand out to Carrie. "Want to dance?"

"Sure, why not?" Carrie said.

Kevin played as Frank and Carrie swirled around the parking lot. Soon more people were gathering around him to listen.

I'm actually performing again, Kevin thought. *Amazing!*

He wished Mary-Kate and Ashley could see him now. But it was a school night, and they had homework to do.

I'll play for them soon, Kevin promised himself. He played a long, soulful note. *In the meantime they're better off with Mrs. Baker. I bet she's keeping them really busy!*

CHAPTER THIRTEEN

"Great! Here's Mrs. Baker's knitting," Mary-Kate said out loud as she rummaged through Mrs. Baker's house. Talking to herself made being there a little less scary.

She picked up the knitting from the sofa. "Mr. Fillmore was holding these needles just before he—before he disappeared. Now if I could just find more evidence . . ."

Mary-Kate glanced around the living room for another clue. Her eyes fell on a box of large plastic trash bags.

"Bingo!" Mary-Kate whispered. "These are just like the bag Mrs. Baker was carrying to the garbage this morning."

But just as she was about to grab the box, she heard the sound of keys rattling in the front door!

Mary-Kate stood frozen with fear. Then she heard her sister's voice filling the house.

"Well, Mrs. Baker!" Ashley was shouting. "Here we are at your front door! Ready to come into your house. Ready or not, here we come!"

Oh, no! Mary-Kate thought. *Mrs. Baker is here. I have to hide!*

Still clutching the knitting, Mary-Kate ducked behind the heavy drapes. When she peeked out, she saw Ashley and Mrs. Baker enter the living room.

"Well!" Ashley shouted. "Here we are in your house. Let's see if we can find your knitting needles!"

"Ashley," Mrs. Baker said. She pointed to her right ear. "You don't have to yell. You're on my good side."

Mary-Kate held her breath as Mrs. Baker looked around the living room.

"That's funny," Mrs. Baker said. "I thought I left my knitting right here on the sofa."

Ashley doesn't know I'm behind the drapes, Mary-Kate thought. *I have to get her attention.*

Mary-Kate waited until Mrs. Baker was on her hands and knees, searching under the sofa. Then she stuck her hand out from behind the drapes.

Waving frantically, Mary-Kate finally caught Ashley's attention.

"Get out!" Ashley mouthed, pointing to the door. "Get out, now!"

Very carefully Mary-Kate slipped out from behind the drapes. She took about three steps when Mrs. Baker stood up.

"Rats!" Mary-Kate whispered under her breath. She slipped back behind the drapes. Her legs felt like jelly as she peeked out.

"No, it's not here," Mrs. Baker said.

"Are those your knitting needles?" Ashley asked. She pointed to the floor. "Over there?"

Mrs. Baker turned her back to the drapes.

"Where?" she asked.

Mary-Kate had little time to act. She darted out from her hiding place and scurried across the living room.

"I don't see anything," Mrs. Baker said. She was about to turn around, when Mary-Kate plunged behind a big chair. "What was that?" she asked.

"Don't worry about the noise, Mrs. Baker," Ashley said. "It was probably just the cat."

"I don't have a cat!" Mrs. Baker said.

"Well, then you might want to call an exterminator!" Ashley said quickly. "Mice can get pretty big these days!"

Mrs. Baker shrugged. She began looking on the floor.

Now! Mary-Kate thought. She crept around the chair on her hands and knees.

"I still can't find them," Mrs. Baker said, checking under the flowered rug.

"Maybe they're in your bedroom!" Ashley suggested.

Mary-Kate inched her way to the door.

"I don't think so," Mrs. Baker said. "I made a New Year's resolution not to knit in bed. Or was it . . . not to eat crackers. Oh, well, I'll check anyway."

Yes! Mary-Kate cheered to herself as Mrs. Baker walked up the stairs toward the bedroom.

The twins ran to each other in the middle of the living room.

"It worked!" Mary-Kate said.

"Quick!" Ashley said. She held out her hands. "Give me the knitting and get out of here!"

"But the knitting needles are our best evidence!" Mary-Kate cried. "They're probably crawling with fingerprints!"

"Listen to me!" Ashley shook Mary-Kate's shoulders. "If Mrs. Baker finds you, you'll end up like poor Mr. Fillmore. Is that what you want, Mary-Kate?"

Mary-Kate was about to answer when Mrs. Baker's voice called from upstairs: "They're not here, Ashley!"

Mary-Kate loosened her grip. Ashley grabbed the knitting needles.

"They've got to be in the living room!" Mrs. Baker shouted down.

Mary-Kate could hear Mrs. Baker's footsteps coming down the stairs. Frantically she glanced around for another place to hide. Next to her there was a round telephone table draped with a long tablecloth.

"Hurry, Mary-Kate!" Ashley whispered.

Mary-Kate slid under the table.

Wow, she thought. *This is harder than stealing bases in softball!*

"Here's your knitting, Mrs. Baker!" Mary-Kate heard Ashley say. "Now, can we go home? I'm starting to miss Mary-Kate. It's one of those twin things!"

"I understand," Mrs. Baker said sweetly. "Of course we can go."

Mary-Kate lifted the tablecloth and peeked out. She could see Mrs. Baker taking the knitting from Ashley's hands.

"Wait a minute," Mrs. Baker said, looking at the yarn attached to the needles. "This thread is leading across the room!"

Mary-Kate looked down at her hands. *Oh, no! She was still holding the ball of yarn!*

She had a sick feeling in her stomach. There was nowhere to run. And nowhere left to hide!

"Why, it's leading to the telephone table!" Mrs. Baker said. "What's going on, Ashley?"

"Nothing, Mrs. Baker!" Ashley said.

Mary-Kate let go of the ball of yarn and gently pushed it out from under the table

Mrs. Baker yanked up the tablecloth.

"Aha!" she cried. "I knew I didn't have mice. What are you doing under here, Mary-Kate?"

Mary-Kate scrambled out from under the table.

"Well, I was just going. Nice to see you, Mrs. Baker!"

But as Mary-Kate headed for the door, Mrs. Baker called out in a frosty voice, "You stop right there, young lady!"

Mary-Kate froze next to Ashley.

"What kind of game are you two playing?" Mrs. Baker asked, waving her knitting needles.

Mary-Kate stared at the knitting needles. Their sharp points glistened in the light.

"Don't hurt us, Mrs. Baker!" Mary-Kate pleaded.

"Hurt you?" Mrs. Baker asked. "Why on earth would I hurt you?"

"Because we know too much!" Ashley wailed.

Just then the living room door swung open. Mary-Kate and Ashley turned around—and gasped.

"Ashley, look!" Mary-Kate cried. "It—it's—"

Ashley gulped. "It's Mr. Fillmore!"

CHAPTER FOURTEEN

"Hello, girls!" Mr. Fillmore said. He smiled at Mrs. Baker. "Hello, Enid."

Ashley stared. Was Mr. Fillmore real—or was he a ghost?

Mary-Kate began to shake. "We thought you were—we thought you were—"

"I know, I know," Mr. Fillmore sighed as he dropped a suitcase on the floor. "You thought I was in Florida. But the airport has been fogged in all day." He put his arm around Mrs. Baker's shoulder.

"I tried to call, but you forgot to leave the answering machine on," he told her.

"Florida?" Ashley asked.

Mary-Kate looked Mr. Fillmore up and down.

"So that means you're not—"

"You're not going!" Mrs. Baker cried happily.

"One of these days," Mr. Fillmore sighed. "But honestly, Enid, I'd much rather stay here with you!"

"Oh, Henry!" Mrs. Baker beamed at him.

"Oh, thank goodness!" Mary-Kate exclaimed as she and Ashley collapsed against each other.

Ashley was relieved, but still confused. If Mrs. Baker didn't kill Mr. Fillmore, what about the weird scene at the window last night?

Just then Mr. Fillmore took the knitting needles from Mrs. Baker's hands.

"Enid!" he said sternly. He began waving the knitting needles in the air. "You know you're not supposed to be knitting. It's bad for your arthritis!"

"Phooey!" Mrs. Baker said. "If I can slice a loaf of pumpernickel, surely I can knit a pair of long johns!"

"Knitting needles?" Ashley said.

"We argue about knitting constantly!" Mrs. Baker said. "It's the one fly in the ointment of our love!" She glanced at Mr. Fillmore. "That and Henry's sister. She lives in Florida."

Mr. Fillmore gave Mrs. Baker's shoulders a squeeze. He frowned at Mary-Kate and Ashley. "What are you girls doing here, anyway?" he asked.

Ashley didn't want to tell Mrs. Baker and Mr. Fillmore the real reason. So she came up with something else.

"Mary-Kate was just trying to hide Mrs. Baker's knitting," Ashley said quickly. "So her arthritis wouldn't get worse."

Mary-Kate grinned at her sister.

"That's it!" she said quickly. "I mean, yeah— exactly."

"Well, thank you, girls," Mrs. Baker said. "I'm very touched." She narrowed her eyes behind her glasses. "Even though I don't quite believe it."

Mary-Kate and Ashley looked at each other.

"Now," Mrs. Baker said. "Let me make Mr. Fillmore something to eat. Then we'll go back to your house. Come, Henry."

After they left the living room, Ashley turned to Mary-Kate.

"Mr. Fillmore looks pretty good," she said, grinning. "You can hardly tell that just yesterday he was chopped up into tiny pieces and stuffed into a garbage can."

Mary-Kate shrugged. "He could have been."

"Mary-Kate!" Ashley protested. "Only a fool would think Mrs. Baker could hurt anybody!"

"Oh, yeah?" Mary-Kate put her hands on her

hips. "Then what are you doing here?"

Ashley gave it a thought. Then she sighed.

"I guess I'm a fool, too," she said. "But I was also worried about you."

"Thanks for covering for me!" Mary-Kate said, smiling.

The twins sat down side by side on Mrs. Baker's sofa. After a few seconds Mary-Kate turned to Ashley.

"Do you think it's too late to renew our pact?" she asked.

"Our pact?" Ashley asked.

"Our no-snooping pact!" Mary-Kate said. "You know, telescopes, notebooks, keyholes, Christmas presents, diaries—"

"Diaries?" Ashley cried. "Mary-Kate, have you been snooping through my diary, too?"

"Only kidding!" Mary-Kate laughed. "But don't think I wasn't tempted!"

Ashley leaned back and smiled. Things were pretty hairy for a while, but in the end everything turned out great. Mr. Fillmore was alive and kicking—and Mrs. Baker was not a killer.

Now, if they could just get her to bake a batch of those killer brownies!

The next morning was Saturday. Kevin was

doing research at the library, so the twins shared breakfast with Carrie. They also shared their secret about Mrs. Baker!

"I still can't believe you thought Mrs. Baker murdered Mr. Fillmore!" Carrie laughed.

"And I can't believe that Dad played the saxophone in front of an audience last night!" Ashley said.

"Maybe next time we can sell tickets," Mary-Kate suggested.

"Great!" Carrie said. "Then you can help me pay for having my car towed."

The back door opened and Max walked in. He was groaning and shaking his head.

"Hi, Carrie," he said. "Hi, Mary-Kate. Ashley."

Ashley smiled at Mary-Kate. Max looked miserable—but at least he was speaking to them again!

"Hi, Max," Ashley said. "Want some scrambled eggs and toast?"

Max sank into a chair. "No, thanks. I'm not very hungry."

"What's up?" Mary-Kate asked.

"Girls!" Max sighed. "You can't live with 'em, and you can't live without 'em."

"What happened?" Carrie asked.

"Ever since Courtney found out I liked her, she

began to like *me*!" Max explained.

"Really?" Mary-Kate gasped.

"Max, that's awesome!" Ashley said. She couldn't believe that Max actually had a girlfriend!

"You mean *awful*!" Max cried. "Courtney and I have been seeing each other for one day and already she wants to study with me! She wants to ride her bike with me! She even wants to come to all of my softball games!"

"Sounds like she's really stuck on you," Carrie said.

"Yeah," Max muttered. "Like those rubber cockroaches you throw against the wall!"

There was a loud knock at the door. Courtney Russell poked her head in.

"There you are, Max!" Courtney said, smiling. She stepped into the kitchen. "I've been looking all over for you!"

"W-w-why?" Max asked.

"Keisha has a new computer," Courtney said. "I thought we could try it out together."

Max sank lower and lower into his chair.

"After that we can walk my dog in the park," Courtney went on. "Max just loves to chase squirrels."

"Arrrgh!" Max groaned.

"And don't forget the book fair this afternoon. And the movies tomorrow, and—"

As Courtney pulled Max out the door, he called over his shoulder: "Trust me! Having a girlfriend just isn't worth the trouble!"

The twins and Carrie stared at the door as it slammed shut.

"You know what else isn't worth the trouble?" Ashley asked.

"What?" Carrie asked.

"Snooping!" Ashley answered.

"That's for sure," Mary-Kate groaned. "From now on, our telescope is permanently aimed toward outer space!"

"Oh, well," Carrie said. "I guess you girls will just have to find another hobby."

"The mall!" Ashley declared.

"Softball!" Mary-Kate cried.

Ashley laughed along with Mary-Kate. Whatever they decided to do would be great.

As long as they did it together!

It all started when we got a new telescope—and decided
to check out our neighbors instead of checking out the
stars. We discovered that people do the weirdest things—
even on Dearborn Street!

Dad found out
and told us to
stop snooping . . .

... but it was much too
fun to stop!

Then things got out of control. We peered through Mrs. Baker's window—and thought we saw Mrs. Baker and Mr. Fillmore having a terrible fight.

Then Mary-Kate
decided that Mr.
Fillmore had
disappeared.
What did
Mrs. Baker do
with him?

That very night Dad hired Mrs. Baker to baby-sit for us! Were we locked in the house with a . . . murderer?

We had to find out. So Mary-Kate sneaked into Mrs. Baker's house to look for clues about what happened to Mr. Fillmore—and was caught red-handed!

Boy, were we embarrassed! We couldn't believe
what we found—Mr. Fillmore! Alive and well and
back from a trip to Florida. Now everything is
back to normal again.

That is, as normal as it gets around here!

PSST! Take a sneak peek
at

My Sister the Supermodel

Ashley hurried down the hallway. Today *Real Teen* magazine was coming to her school to choose models for their new fashion issue, and she didn't want to be late. Ashley was *sure* she would be picked. She was born to be a model!

Wait till they see how fabulous I look, she thought. She smoothed down her light blue slip-dress. It had beading at the top and she wore high platform shoes to match. Her hair was exactly the way she liked it best—piled on her head, with lots of pieces twisted into crazy loops.

Her friend Jennifer was waiting for Ashley by her locker. She was dressed in a slinky black dress, three rhinestone necklaces, and stacked heels.

"They're doing the tryouts first thing this morning!" Jennifer squealed.

"Cool!" Ashley answered, grabbing her friend's hand.

"I got our passes from Mr. Morrow, so we don't even have to go to class," Jennifer explained. "We're in the first group."

"That's great—thanks," Ashley said. "I am so ready for this."

The two of them hurried to the west wing hallway, where the *Real Teen* tryouts were being held.

A famous model named Tara James was there with the photographers. She told each girl where to go and what to do.

Pretty soon, it was Ashley's turn. The photographer used a camcorder to videotape her tryout. Ashley gave him her biggest smile for about half of the poses. For the other half, she arched her back, tossed her head, and tried to look really glamorous.

"That was great!" the photographer said. "Thanks."

"Uh, is that all?" Ashley asked. "What about the shots on the stairway? I saw you doing those with some of the other girls."

"I think we've got all we need, thank you," Tara James said with a nice smile. "We'll put the results on the bulletin board by the end of school today. Good luck."

Okay, Ashley thought. She started to walk away, back toward her homeroom. But just then, Mary-Kate showed up.

"Hold on," Ashley whispered to Jennifer. "I want to watch Mary-Kate try out."

"What for?"Jennifer snapped. "She doesn't have a prayer."

"She *is* my twin, you know!" Ashley argued, sticking up for her sister.

"Please," Jennifer moaned. "There's no comparison. You know how to dress. How to walk. How to *everything!* She knows how to shoot a—what do you call it—layout shot on the basketball court."

"A layup," Ashley corrected her.

She watched for a minute as Mary-Kate posed for the photographers. Mary-Kate gave them a sweet smile each time they asked for it. But she didn't strut or twirl or anything.

Come on, Mary-Kate, Ashley coached her silently. *Lift your chin! Swing your hips!*

Ashley waved her hands to try to get Mary-Kate's attention.

But Mary-Kate just ignored her.

Jennifer's right, Ashley decided. *Mary-Kate doesn't have a chance of being picked for the fashion shoot.*

She just didn't have the fashion look that said:

"Wear what I wear. Do what I do. Copy me."

"Come on," Ashley said to Jennifer. "Let's go back to class."

But Jennifer wasn't quite ready to leave.

She marched up to Tara. "I just want to tell you it's been a pleasure working with you," Jennifer gushed. "And I'm looking forward to doing a really spectacular shoot."

"I hope you had a good time on the tryouts," Tara replied.

"Thank you," Jennifer called. Then she tossed in the Italian word for goodbye. *"Ciao!"*

"Laying it on a little thick, aren't you?" Ashley asked, rolling her eyes.

"I just wanted to let her know that when she picks me, she'll be working with a professional. Someone who speaks her language," Jennifer explained. Then she headed down the hall toward their homeroom. "Now all we have to do is wait!"

Right, Ashley thought. *Wait. All day until three o'clock. How can I stand it?* she wondered. *Today is going to be the longest day of my life!*

"This is it!" Ashley declared as she and Mary-Kate hurried from their sixth-period class. "The start of my lifetime career as a model. But don't worry. I won't forget the little people—the ones I knew on my way to the top."

She patted Mary-Kate on the head when she said "little people." Then she laughed, because it was true. Even though they were twins, Ashley was just a bit taller than her sister. And she looked a lot taller today, since she was wearing platform shoes and Mary-Kate wasn't.

"Give me a break," Mary-Kate complained. "On your way to the top of what?"

"The modeling world, of course," Ashley replied. "But don't worry. I won't forget you when I get there. Come on—let's go see the list."

Ashley pushed her way through the crowded school hallway toward the main bulletin board. That's where the Fashion Van would post the list of kids who were chosen for the photo shoot.

But when she got to the hall, she couldn't get close enough to the board to read the piece of paper. The hallway was packed with kids clamoring to see who was going to be in the magazine fashion lay-out.

Wow, Ashley thought, glancing around. *Even kids who didn't try out are hanging out here!*

Then she smiled to herself. *They probably just*

want to be around us, she decided. *So they can tell their friends, "I knew Ashley Burke when . . ."*

"There's Jennifer," Mary-Kate said, giving Ashley a nudge and pointing toward the front of the crowd. "Hey, Jennifer. Did they pick you?" Mary-Kate called.

"For that stupid photo layout?" Jennifer said angrily. "Who cares?"

"Whoa," Mary-Kate murmured to Ashley. "Sounds like she tanked."

Well, I'm not surprised, Ashley thought, trying to stay calm and be reasonable. *They can't choose too many girls who are totally beautiful and have attitude— like me. And like Jennifer. They probably didn't want us all to look alike!*

Still, Ashley started to feel a little bit nervous and jumpy in her stomach.

Jennifer was supercool. And her fashion sense was perfect. If she didn't get picked . . . would Ashley?

Ashley pushed a little harder, trying to wedge her way through the crowd to the bulletin board. One by one, the kids at the front read the list and then turned away.

Finally it was Ashley's turn.

"Well?" Mary-Kate called from off to the side.

"Did you make it, Ashley?"

Ashley's mouth dropped open. She couldn't believe what she was seeing. But there it was—in big black letters typed on the white page.

Mary-Kate Burke.

Her twin sister's name was on the list—but hers wasn't!

"Did you make it?" Mary-Kate called again, a little louder this time.

"No," Ashley sputtered, pushing her way out of the crowd. "But you did."

HANG OUT
WITH
MARY-KATE & ASHLEY
in their brand-new book series

BASED ON THE HIT ABC-TV SERIES!

COLLECT THEM ALL!

**VISIT Mary-Kate & Ashley on their website—
www.marykateandashley.com**

At bookstores everywhere, or
call 1-800-331-3761 to order.   HarperEntertainment

 PARACHUTE PRESS   DUALSTAR PUBLICATIONS

TWO OF A KIND TM & © 1999 Warner Bros.

PSSST —The Secret's Out!

The Trenchcoat Twins™ Are Solving Brand-New Mysteries!

VISIT Mary-Kate & Ashley on their Web site— www.marykateandashley.com

The New Adventures of MARY-KATE & ASHLEY

The Case Of The GREAT ELEPHANT ESCAPE

The Case Of The SUMMER CAMP CAPER

The Case Of The Surfing Secret

The Case Of The GREEN GHOST

The Case Of The

READ THEM ALL!

At bookstores everywhere, or call 1-800-331-3761 to order.

HarperEntertainment
A Division of HarperCollins*Publishers*
www.harpercollins.com

The New Adventures of Mary-Kate & Ashley TM & © 1999 Dualstar Entertainment Group, Inc.

PARACHUTE PRESS   DUALSTAR PUBLICATIONS

High Above Hollywood Mary-Kate & Ashley Are Playing Matchmakers!

Check Them Out in Their Coolest New Movie

Mary-Kate Olsen

Ashley Olsen

Billboard DAD

One's a surfer. The other's a high diver. When these two team up to find a new love for their single Dad by taking out a personals ad on a billboard in the heart of Hollywood, it's a fun-loving, eye-catching California adventure gone wild!

Now on Video!

DUALSTAR VIDEO

TM & © 1999 Dualstar Entertainment Group, Inc. Distributed by Warner Home Video, 4000 Warner Blvd., Burbank, CA 91522. Printed in USA. All rights reserved. Billboard Dad and all logos, character names and other distinctive likenesses thereof are the trademarks of Dualstar Entertainment Group, Inc. Design and Photography © 1999 Dualstar Entertainment Group, Inc. and Warner Home Video.

Look for the best-selling detective home video episodes.

The Case Of The Volcano Adventure™
The Case Of The U.S. Navy Mystery™
The Case Of The Hotel Who•Done•It™
The Case Of The Shark Encounter™
The Case Of The U.S. Space Camp® Mission™
The Case Of The Fun House Mystery™
The Case Of The Christmas Caper™
The Case Of The Sea World® Adventure™
The Case Of The Mystery Cruise™
The Case Of The Logical i Ranch™
The Case Of Thorn Mansion™

Join the fun!

You're Invited To Mary-Kate & Ashley's™ Costume Party™ **NEW**
You're Invited To Mary-Kate & Ashley's™ Mall Party™ **NEW**
You're Invited To Mary-Kate & Ashley's™ Camp Out Party™
You're Invited To Mary-Kate & Ashley's™ Ballet Party™
You're Invited To Mary-Kate & Ashley's™ Birthday Party™
You're Invited To Mary-Kate & Ashley's™ Christmas Party™
You're Invited To Mary-Kate & Ashley's™ Sleepover Party™
You're Invited To Mary-Kate & Ashley's™ Hawaiian Beach Party™

And also available:

Mary-Kate and Ashley Olsen: Our Music Video™
Mary-Kate and Ashley Olsen: Our First Video™

DUALSTAR
VIDEO

TM & ©1999 Dualstar Entertainment Group, Inc.
Distributed by KidVision, a division of Warner Vision Entertainment. All rights reserved.
A Warner Music Group Company.

KidVision
A DIVISION OF
WARNERVISION
ENTERTAINMENT

Don't Miss

Mary-Kate & Ashley

in their 2 newest videos!

Available Now Only on Video.

DUALSTAR VIDEO

www.marykateandashley.com   www.warnerbros.com

KidVision
A DIVISION OF
WARNERVISION
ENTERTAINMENT

TM & ©1999 Dualstar Entertainment Group, Inc. Distributed by Kidvision, a division of WarnerVision Entertainment. A Warner Music Group Company. Printed in the USA. All rights reserved. Dualstar Video, You're Invited To Mary-Kate & Ashley's Costume Party, You're Invited To Mary-Kate & Ashley's Mall Party, Mary-Kate + Ashley's Fun Club, and all logos, character names and other distinctive likenesses thereof are the trademarks of Dualstar Entertainment Group, Inc. Package and art design ©1999 Dualstar Entertainment Group, Inc.

Two Times the Fun!
Two Times the Excitement!
Two Times the Adventure!

Check Out All Eight *You're Invited* Video Titles...

... And All Four Feature-Length Movies!

And Look for Mary-Kate & Ashley's Adventure Video Series.

DUALSTAR VIDEO

TM & © 1999 Dualstar Entertainment Group Inc. Distributed by Warner Home Video. 4000 Warner Blvd. Burbank, CA 91522. Printed in USA. All rights reserved. It Takes Tw How the West Was Fun, You're Invited to Mary-Kate & Ashley's Birthday Party, You're Invite to Mary-Kate & Ashley's Christmas Party, You're Invited to Mary-Kate & Ashley Hawaiian Beach Party, You're Invited to Mary-Kate & Ashley's Sleepover Party, You're Invited to Mary-Kate & Ashley's Ballet Party, You're Invited to Mary-Kate & Ashley's Can Out Party, You're Invited to Mary-Kate & Ashley's Costume Party, You're Invited to Mary-Kate & Ashley's Mall Party and all logos, character names and other distinctive lik nesses thereof are the trademarks of Dualstar Entertainment Group, Inc. Double, Double, Toil and Trouble and To Grandmother's House We Go © Dualstar Productions a Green/Epstein Productions Inc. Design © 1999 Dualstar Entertainment Group, Inc.

Listen To Us!

Ballet Party™

Birthday Party™

Sleepover Party™

Mary-Kate & Ashley's Cassettes and CDs
Available Now Wherever Music is Sold

LIGHTYEAR

Lightyear®
Entertainment

DUALSTAR
RECORDS

TMs & ©℗1997 Dualstar Records.

Distributed
in the
U.S. by

wea

It doesn't matter if you live around the corner...
or around the world....
If you are a fan of Mary-Kate and Ashley Olsen,
you should be a member of

Mary-Kate + Ashley's Fun Club™

Here's what you get
Our Funzine™
An autographed color photo
Two black and white individual photos
A full sized color poster
An official Fun Club™ membership card
A Fun Club™ School folder
Two special Fun Club™ surprises
Fun Club™ Collectible Catalog
Plus a Fun Club™ box to keep everything in.

To join Mary-Kate + Ashley's Fun Club™, fill out the form below
and send it along with

U.S. Residents	$17.00
Canadian Residents	$22.00 (US Funds only)
International Residents	$27.00 (US Funds only)

Mary-Kate + Ashley's Fun Club™
859 Hollywood Way, Suite 275
Burbank, CA 91505

Name:_____

Address:_____

City:_____ St:_____ Zip:_____

Phone: (_____) _____

E-Mail:_____

Check us out on the web at
www.marykateandashley.com

© & TM 1999 Dualstar Entertainment Group, Inc